BECKY

THE THROAT GOAT

IN THE LAND WHERE
HORNY GOATS DWELL

LIVES A LADY WITH A
TALE TO TELL

BECKY THE THROAT GOAT,
IS ALWAYS FUN

WHEN SHE GOES OUT,
EVERYBODY COMES

BORN WITH AN OVERSIZED
THROAT SO GRAND

A RARE CONDITION
SHE NEVER PLANNED

SWALLOWING OBJECTS
WITH THE GREATEST OF EASE

HER PRESENCE AT PARTIES,
ALWAYS A TEASE

SHE'LL TAKE THINGS DOWN,
BOTH LARGE AND SMALL

BECKY THE THROAT GOAT,
SWALLOWS IT ALL

THE MALE GOATS ALWAYS, ERUPTING WITH LAUGHTER

BUT A DATE WITH BECKY,
IS WHAT THEY'RE AFTER

THEY CALL UP BECKY,
AND RUN THEIR PLAYS

BECAUSE A NIGHT WITH THE THROAT GOAT LEAVES THEM IN A DAZE

I have over 100 humor books and several strange coloring books available on Amazon.

My humor books cover a wide range of topics and styles, from dumb jokes and puns to satirical takes on current events. Whatever your sense of humor, you'll find something to love or hate in my collection.

And for those who want to tap into their creative side, my strange coloring books offer unique and unconventional designs for you to color in and make your own. These books are perfect for relaxing after a long day, or for getting in touch with your inner artist.

So don't wait any longer to add some laughter and creativity to your life. Check out my other books on Amazon today!

Here are just a few...

books.bradgosse.com

MIKE HUNT
SMELLS LIKE FISH

Clap along with Mike Hunt. This book is filled with hilarious double entendres. You know what it's about. Don't make me spell it out for you. This book is cheap as balls. Like your mom.

MIKE LIT
Shouldn't Be Hard To Find

Only $10

Every girl, and some guys want my big black hawk. This book teaches you why big black hawks matter.

ALL THE GIRLS LOVE
MY BIG BLACK HAWK

CUCUMBER CURTIS

Can't come to dinner. Your mom has other plans for this innocent little vegetable.

GLUCK GLUCK 3000

Sex Robots are the new wave of the future in sexual entertainment. In fact, they're already in the process of being built. Catering to the needs of lonely men and women, these bots will soon be ubiquitous.

SEXTOY STORY

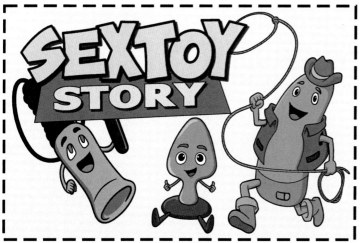

RACE WARS

Black, car, white car, and yellow car too.

STD'S & YOU

Learning From The Animals At The Zoo

CONJOINED TWINS
Where Does One End and The Other Begin?

What if one can swim and the other can not? Can just one of them become an astronaut? How often do they need a diaper change? If they grew 100 feet tall wouldn't that be strange? Are they a by-product of nuclear radiation? Have they ever been left outside a fire station?

LEARN ABOUT INBREEDING WITH
DONKEYBEAR

Are your parents cousins or siblings? This book will teach you all about inbreeding. You can learn along with Donkeybear. He's hearing about it for the first time.

MOM RUNS TRAINS
On The Weekend With Dad's Friends

It's career day at school. And I get to present. I'm so proud of my mom. And the weekends she's spent. Learning to run trains.

SANTAS LIL HUMPER
SAVES CHRISTMAS

Santa crashes in the Middle East and Rudolf is dead. Only a strange camel can save Christmas now.

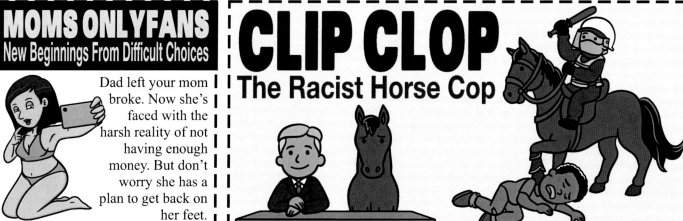

MOMMY GOT A DUI

Your mom has secrets. She hides her drinking from you… Until now. Mommy can't drive you to school and you're going to have to learn the bus routes.

INSOMNIAC & FRIENDS
The Clowns That Put You To Sleep

Yeetyeet likes to watch you sleep. Pickles under your bed he creeps. Switchblade eats your favorite stuffies. Pedo lures you away with puppies. Shifty plans to collect your teeth. Twisty smells your hair while you sleep. Clammy lives inside his van. Hank once had to kill a man. Tooty smells your dirty socks. Busby laughs at electric shocks. Twinkles spends the night robbing graves. Fappy keeps a few human slaves.

MY RACIST GRAN

WHY DADDY HITS MOMMY

A Kids Guide To Understanding Alcoholism

DEAD BABIES
COLORING BOOKS

TRIGGERED
Kids Guide To Cancel Culture

Easily offended is the new trend. People act outraged. Be careful, you might lose your job. Even though nobody is responsible for the feelings of others.

OK BOOMER

Boomer always complains at the store. But it was on sale yesterday!! When yesterday's special isn't available anymore. You shouldn't be such a slut. Boomer gives unsolicited advice. This smart phone is dumber than dirt. Boomer always struggles with his device. Boomer demands your supervisor.

CANDIS NUTS
Come In The Morning Each Day

MELT IN YOUR MOUTH

CINNAMON

A horse forced into the sex trade.

Only $10

DON'T BATHE WITH UNCLE JOE
Setting Boundaries With Adults

Uncle Joe lost his job. For misconduct in the workplace. He's coming to stay with us. You're going to have to learn to avoid his hands and more importantly. NEVER bathe with uncle Joe.

THIRST TRAPS

Why Moms Phone Keeps Blowing Up

DADDY'S A SIMP

Don't Expect Much Inheritance

HUMPTY DUMPTY

Discovers Workplace Misconduct

Made in United States
Orlando, FL
01 September 2023

36603230R00015